Keen Teens

Volume 1

The Dance Company
Jonathan Caren

Flip Turn
Madeleine George

A Polar Bear in New Jersey
Anna Moench

A SAMUEL FRENCH ACTING EDITION

FOUNDED 1830

SAMUELFRENCH.COM
SAMUELFRENCH-LONDON.CO.UK

FOR PRODUCTION ENQUIRIES

UNITED STATES AND CANADA
Info@SamuelFrench.com
1-866-598-8449

UNITED KINGDOM AND EUROPE
Plays@SamuelFrench-London.co.uk
020-7255-4302

Each title is subject to availability from Samuel French, depending upon country of performance. Please be aware that *THE DANCE COMPANY, FLIP TURN, AND A POLAR BEAR IN NEW JERSEY* may not be licensed by Samuel French in your territory. Professional and amateur producers should contact the nearest Samuel French office or licensing partner to verify availability.

MUSIC USE NOTE

IMPORTANT BILLING AND CREDIT REQUIREMENTS

FOREWORD

I fell in love with the theater in high school. Upon being cast in a play, I gained access to the secret language of the art form—the vocabulary, the protocol, the superstitions. Did we really tell one another to break a leg? Woe would be upon us, upperclasspersons warned, if we allowed an audience member to glimpse us in costume in the hallway before or during the performance. Most importantly, we learned that we'd made a serious commitment—to our ensemble, to our director, to the audience, and to the work.

Working with teenagers today, I'm happy to report that the love they feel for the theater is the same as it ever was. Unfortunately, according to a survey by the Educational Theatre Association, so are the plays. Nine of the ten full-length most-performed plays in high schools are at least 50 years old. While the works of legendary writers—Shakespeare, Miller, Wilder, Kaufman and Hart—are alive and well in high schools, nowhere on this list do we see the great dramatists of our time.

And quite a time it is. According to André Bishop, the artistic director of Lincoln Center Theater, "we are currently living in a golden age of American playwriting, though we may not realize it or even want to admit it." As a director working with new plays, I experience André's statement as the unvarnished truth every day. But how might a high school student—versed in worthy, but long-toothed material—learn about our golden age of dramatic writing?

It is not an easy problem to solve. In too many schools, the arts are perceived as a luxury, rather than central to our experience as human beings. Many great plays produced on Broadway and in regional theaters won't be performed by students—their cast sizes are just too small; an era of political polarization has ensured that other popular plays won't find their way to students because of leery, even censorious administrators. But the kids are still all right—and they still love the theater in the way that I did.

Luckily for me, I work for the great Keen Company, which is as committed to new work for young people as we are to our off-Broadway productions. Since 2007, we've been bringing great professional playwrights together with young actors from New York City and the surrounding environs. Our Keen Teens program commissions work for high schools that involves a large cast and reflects Keen Company's mission of producing theater that provokes identification, reflection and emotional connection. Keen Teens plays provide an opportunity for high school students to engage deeply and honestly with the world around then.

In this volume, you'll find the collected plays from our seventh season. In Jonathan Caren's *The Dance Company*, three high school football players infiltrate an all-girl dance company and we see very different versions of how it all went down. Madeleine George's *Flip Turn* takes us underwater at a public pool, where an ordinary day calls for extraordinary feats of daring and trust. In *A Polar Bear in New Jersey*, by Anna Moench, global warming forces a teenage polar bear out of her comfortable habit and into...New Jersey.

We hope you'll read, enjoy and produce these plays, so great work by contemporary playwrights can be seen and heard by high school students everywhere. Some of them might even fall in love.

– Mark Armstrong
Director of New Work
Keen Company

Special Thanks:

Blake Lawrence and Playscripts, Inc, who created Keen Teens in 2007 and nurtured it in the years that followed; Larissa Lury, 2013's Program Director, who led the teens so wonderfully; and the families of the casts.

Keen Company would like to thank the following Keen Teens Angels for their generous support of Keen Teens: Cathy and Robert Altholz, Harrison and Leslie Bains, Amy and Brad Ball, George and Jane Bean, Jeff and Tina Bolton, George Boyer, Bill and Casey Bradford, Kathleen Chalfant, Buena Chilstrom, Rose Courtney and Ned Benkert, Jocelyn Cushing, Brian d'Arcy James and Jennifer Prescott, Linda D'Onofrio, Kate and Steve Davis, Lucy and Nat Day, Ted and Lynn Doll, Anne T. Fitzgerald, Patricia Follert, Ray and Cathy Garea, Christine Gentile, Timothy Grandia, Albert R. and Molly Gurney, Jennifer Jahn, Missy and Ed Kelly, David and Kate Kies, Anki Leeds, Marsha Mason, Donna and Jack McCoy, Erik Piecuch, Carol Quint, Gail and Charles Rubinger, Vincent Smith and Alice Silkworth, Mike Emmerman and Pat Stockhausen, Barry Waldorf and Stan Gotlin, Alban Wilson, Ernest and Judith Wong.

The Dance Company

Jonathan Caren

THE DANCE COMPANY premiered with Keen Company (Jonathan Silverstein, Artistic Director), as part of Keen Teens Season 7, at Theatre Row in New York City on May 3, 2013. The performance was directed by Jonathen Caren, with sets by Collin McGurk, costumes by Amanda Jenks, lighting by Jeffrey Toombs, and sound by Colin Whitely. The Production Stage Manager was Alex H. Hajjar. The cast was as follows:

JOIE	Christine Garmendiz
GUZMAN	Ralphie Irizarry
AMANDA	Zoë Marcel
JAZ	Tori Matos
LEO	Oddisey Miller
ELENA	Maheen Naz
LIZ	Elsie Razo
SARAH	Nyasa Robinson
JESSIE	Angel Rodriguez
MAYA	Ariadne Vasquez

CHARACTERS

JOIE
GUZMAN
AMANDA
JAZ
LEO
ELENA
LIZ
SARAH
JESSIE
MAYA

SETTING

A rehearsal room. An auditorium stage.

TIME

Now

Scene One

*(On a bare stage: The Dance Company stretches to warm-up music. Stage left, **AMANDA** busts a move. Stage right, **ELINA** tries to one-up her. **AMANDA** tries to one-up that. It becomes heated, competitive until they address the audience. They will be our narrators throughout.)*

AMANDA. This is The Dance Company.

ELINA. *The Advanced* Dance Company of Northern Academy.

AMANDA. We're an elite company of dancers.

ELINA. In case you're wondering it is we do?

AMANDA. We dance.

*(**AMANDA** strikes a pose. So does **ELINA**. They vogue.)*

ELINA. Ballet. Modern. Hip Hop.

AMANDA. We do it.

ELINA. And?

AMANDA. We do it well.

ELINA. But it's hard to get in.

AMANDA. Seriously. Not everyone gets in.

*(**MAYA** checks a list pinned to a wall. She SCREAMS.)*

ELINA. Relax. That's last year's list.

AMANDA. Seriously. You have *no* idea how hard I worked to get in. I worked *so* hard. I didn't *sleep*, I didn't *eat*, like – *gluten.*

ELINA. Amanda.

AMANDA. Anyway. This year things got even more competitive.

ELINA. And not just over who was front and center for the finale.

(**LEO** *arrives at the studio. He looks lost. Confused.*)

LEO. Excuse me?

(The dancers all stop. Music cuts out.)

MAYA. Can I help you?

LEO. Where do I go to audition for The Dance Company?

*(Actors freeze in places, except for **ELINA** and **AMANDA**.)*

ELINA. Wait that's like not how it went down at all.

AMANDA. He was a *natural.*

ELINA. He was a jock.

AMANDA. You have to admit. He had funk.

ELINA. If you're referring to his body odor.

AMANDA. Is there anything we can agree on?

ELINA. Um. This guy was a major –

AMANDA & ELINA. Aaaaa-thlete.

ELINA. Take it back. I'll tell it. Five. Six. Seven. Eight…

(Dancers rewind and re-take their places. A new song plays. Something up tempo. Hip hop.)

ELINA. Aw yeah. That's more like it.

*(**LEO** walks in with brazen confidence.)*

SARAH MASTERS. Can I help you?

LEO. Yeah. Where do I go to audition for The Dance Company?

LIZ. *You* want to audition for Dance Company?

LEO. Is that a problem?

(Freeze. Music goes out.)

AMANDA. Ok ok ok hold up.

ELINA. What?

AMANDA. He did *not* shimmy in like he invented the Cincinnati.

ELINA. Whatever. He's your hotdog. Just don't like embellish the relish.

AMANDA. His name was Leo. And he was a definitely a DiCaprio.

LIZ. What makes you want to audition for The Dance Company?

(Everyone frozen. Spotlight on AMANDA.*)*

LEO. I'm in love with Amanda. I've been watching her dance since freshman year. They way she does her arabesques. How her torso stays upright while she pliés. Amanda, you had me at third position.

*(*LEO *freezes.)*

ELINA. Amanda!

AMANDA. So he didn't know who I was.

ELINA. Or anything about dance.

AMANDA. What Leo knew was Beavers.

ELINA. The Beaver was our school mascot.

AMANDA. And he was captain of the football team. So he knew a thing or two about them.

(Unfreeze. LIZ *approaches* LEO.*)*

LIZ. I'm Liz. Assistant choreographer and Captain of The Dance Company.

LEO. Nice to meet you. I'm Leo.

JOIE. Number 32 for the touchdown, woop woop!

LIZ. Apparently some of us know who you are already.

LEO. *(trying to play it down)* Just what happens when you play sports.

LIZ. Didn't say I did.

LEO. I want to audition for The Dance Company if that's still possible.

LIZ. Do you know anything about movement?

LEO. I know a few moves.

(Cue Gangham Style or some other uptempo song. LEO *attempts to dance but he's not very good. Music cuts out.)*

LEO. OK. So I can't dance. But I want to learn.

LIZ. You realize this is The "Advanced" Dance Company.

MAYA. I've been taking ballet, tap and Jazz *every single weekend* for the past *eight* years.

LIZ. Nine.

JOIE. *Ten*. And a bag of chips….which I'm not allowed to eat.

LIZ. You wouldn't join the football team without knowing how to tackle a wide receiver.

ELINA. We know why you're here, Leo.

MAYA. Why is he here?

(All eyes turn to **SARAH MASTERS**.*)*

MAYA. *(putting one and one together)* Ohhhhh. Why am I always the last one to know everything?

SARAH MASTERS. Leave me out of this.

(Freeze.)

ELINA. Sarah Masters.

AMANDA. Leo used to date Sarah.

ELINA. Date is a loaded word.

AMANDA. I heard they made out after a playoff game.

ELINA. I heard he tried to kiss her and she rejected him.

ELINA. The bottom line was – He was way too full of himself.

AMANDA. *She* was the one who was full of *herself.*

ELINA. Let's just say there was too much fullness going on for one high school relationship.
Unfreeze.

(Unfreeze.)

LEO. I just want to learn how to dance. That's it.

LIZ. Why?

LEO. Because…I can't go back to the football team.

LIZ. Because…

LEO. Because football players are big. And I'm like medium. And when big meets medium on the field, not-so-good things happen for medium.

JOIE. I thought you were *captain.*

LEO. *Of the JV team.* Before everyone went through crazy puberty. I used to bench press 150. Now they bench press me!

(GUZMAN and JESSIE arrive in football pads. GUZMAN is a little slower, bigger, and less coordinated. JESSIE was born to wear a dance belt.)

GUZMAN. One. Two. Three four...

JESSIE. What are you counting?

GUZMAN. How many girls there are in one room!

JESSIE. Coach is asking for you, Leo.

LEO. Tell him I'm not coming back.

GUZMAN. Uh.

LEO. What are you waiting for?

GUZMAN. It's just...Coach is really loud and big and quite frankly I'm afraid of him.

SARAH MASTERS. Go back to football, Leo. No one wants you here.

LEO. Sarah. Can we just talk?

SARAH MASTERS. This is *my* dance company.

JOIE. You mean *"Our* company".

MAYA. Wait. What's so wrong with having a guy in the Dance Company?

SARAH MASTERS. Nothing is *wrong* with it. Except <u>he can't dance</u>.

ELINA. You know what he *can* do? Ruin our chemistry. Don't you see? He's already dividing us.

MAYA. Elina has a point.

SARAH MASTERS. The spring show is in six weeks. How can he learn to dance in that amount of time?

AMANDA. But Jaz was practically begging us to recruit a few guys so we could do lifts –

(ELINA covers AMANDA's mouth.)

LEO. Look. I'm not here to ruin your chemistry. But I am fast and I'm strong and I'm a quick learner so… I'm yours if you'll have me.

GOTTLEIB. Show them your touchdown dance.

LEO. C'mon, Guzman. These are like *real* dancers.

JESSIE. I'll show them mine!

(JESSIE does an elaborate post touchdown dance. He goes really far with it. It morphs into some serious modern movement. He's fantastic.)

JOIE. Whaaaaaaaaaaat.

LEO. OK. I've *never* seen you do *that.*

LIZ. You totally stole that from our spring show.

JESSIE. It's true. I recorded it on my iPhone. And…I may have watched it a few times. Liz, your in-steps are ah-may-zing.

LIZ. OK. I like you.

(Freeze.)

AMANDA. Jessie was good.

ELINA. He was a *brill-cheese sandwich.*

AMANDA. He deserved to be in The Dance Company.

ELINA. He deserved to be in Alvin Ailey.

AMANDA. That's when our choreographer Jaz came back –

(JAZ, the high-octane teacher, barges in.)

JAZ. Everybody, stop! I was just *struck* by inspiration. Literally – on Broadway and 34th. A taxi came flying at me, so I did a quick brise, but my torso hit the windshield. Luckily, I frapped off the glass, flipped in the air and landed in third position. Made it unscathed, but my brain is a little shaken, or I should say "awakened" because an idea came to me for our finale!

(She begins to choreograph. LIZ trails her, mentally memorizing.)

JAZ. It's about trying to survive, yet going with the flow. Accepting what life throws at you, but not backing down. Showing your flair but doing it with composure. Liz, are you getting this?

LIZ. On it.

JAZ. It's going to be raw, sexy, sleek, yet modern and mechanical, with grand sweeping gestures. We're all going to get *emotionally naked here* –

GUZMAN. Wow.

JAZ. – *metaphorically* speaking. With the adrenaline of a taxi, dodging pedestrians. It's the intersection of the two, the confluence and chaos of dance. The sidewalk is our audience. We'll bring the street to the stage. I call it the "Cab Cab-aret".

(*JAZ lands in* **GUZMAN**'s *arms.*)

JESSIE. I want in!

JAZ. Who are these guys?

ELINA. They were just about to leave –

AMANDA. (finishing her sentence) – *it on the dance floor!*

LEO. I'm Leo. This is Jessie and Guzman.

JOIE. They're football players.

JAZ. Jocks?

GUZMAN. I don't really get on the field all that much.

LEO. Guzman's more like the water boy.

GUZMAN. (*feigning enthusiasm*) Yay Beavers.

JESSIE. We want to audition for Dance Company.

JAZ. All of you?

LEO. I know auditions have passed. But if there's anyway we could be of service?

JAZ. This is about *performance*. You have to know what you're doing.

LEO. I've been playing sports my whole life. I can do things. Pivots. Jab steps. Push-ups.

JAZ. Could you catch a girl in the air after a grand ronde jambe en L'aire?

LEO. I have no idea what that means, but I could try.

JAZ. Sarah? Go for it. Land in his arms.

SARAH MASTERS. Do I have to?

JAZ. If you want to be in the front line for "le fin de siècle".

(*SARAH attempts a jump.* **LEO** *catches her. They lock eyes.*)

JAZ. Not bad.

JESSIE. I can do that.

(*JESSIE jumps into* **GUZMAN***'s arms.*)

JESSIE. I was mainly into football for the tights.

GUZMAN. Ok, my arms are getting really tired here.

(**GUZMAN** *drops* **JESSIE***.*)

LEO. If you let us in, we'll work extra hard. Obviously, Jessie's good enough. But Guzman and me? We'll lift whomever you want us to lift.

JAZ. It *would* be fun to choreograph some lifts. Especially for the cab-cabaret.

AMANDA. Told you.

JAZ. I have to run it by the company. What do you think? Should let them in?

(*This could also be addressed to the audience. All the girls raise hands except* **ELINA** *and* **SARAH**. **AMANDA** *pulls* **ELINA***'s hand up.*)

LEO. Sarah.

SARAH. If everyone thinks it'll be good for the company.

(**SARAH** *raises her hand.*)

JAZ. Congratulations. You're in. I'll need some volunteers to catch them up to speed.

AMANDA. *Fine.* I'll do it.

JAZ. Great. Amanda, you help Leo.

LEO. Thanks.

JAZ. Now who wants to help –

GOTTLEIB. Oh uh. It's Guzman.

JAZ. Do you have a first name?

JESSIE. He prefers Guzman.

GUZMAN. I prefer Guzman.

JAZ. OK. Who wants to train Guzman?

GUZMAN. Guzman going once. Guzman going twice.

ELINA. *(a martyr)* I'll do it.

GUZMAN. Thanks.

JAZ. And you're –

JESSIE. Jessie.

JAZ. Jessie's going to co-choreograph with you, Liz.

LIZ. "Awesome".

Scene Two.

Music Transition. Dance Transition.

AMANDA. And just like that, we were breaking them in like a pair of t-split tap shoes.

ELINA. Worst idea in the history of Dance Company.

AMANDA. So they needed a little guidance.

ELINA. And a lesson on how to put on their dance belts.

GUZMAN. Uhhhh. What's a dance belt?

(ELINA whispers to him.)

GUZMAN. Oh.

(She keeps whispering.)

GUZMAN. But where does the little string thing go?

(AMANDA tosses him the dance belt.)

GUZMAN. Man. I'm not entirely confident this thing is going to stay in place.

(GUZMAN starts to take off his pants.)

AMANDA. In the dressing room!

(GUZMAN exits. LEO returns wearing sweats and a t-shirt.)

LEO. Hey!

AMANDA. Hi!

LEO. Ready to rehearse?

AMANDA. Let's do it!

LEO. Is this OK, what I'm wearing?

AMANDA. As long as you can move around comfortably.

LEO. Better than in shoulder pads and a helmet.

AMANDA. So, let's do it.

LEO. Teach me to tango!

AMANDA. Tango is more ballroom.

LEO. That was a general expression.

AMANDA. Ah.

LEO. What I *meant* was, I'm all yours. Do what you want with me! Should we put on some music?

AMANDA. You *really* want to learn how to dance?

LEO. Why is that so hard for everyone to believe?

AMANDA. Not every guy in the world wants to give up football to master a pirouette.

(SARAH walks by.)

SARAH. I forgot my bag.

(SARAH exits.)

LEO. I know what you're thinking.

AMANDA. I didn't say anything.

LEO. I'm not just doing this for Sarah Masters. We've known each other for years. That's all.

AMANDA. Uh huh.

LEO. I mean, obviously she's pretty. And yes, we kissed once after a football game and no she didn't reject me, it was just a little weird and confusing so we mutually agreed not to do it again.

AMANDA. You don't have to justify it to me.

LEO. Look. Don't tell anyone but…Her parents are getting divorced.

AMANDA. Oh.

LEO. Our parents are friends. They used to come over for dinner. Now they don't. Since they split she basically stopped talking to me. So I'm trying to be there for her.

AMANDA. So you joined the dance company just to check with her?

LEO. Yeah. I guess.

AMANDA. Wow. That's very –

LEO. Stalker?

AMANDA. I was going to say, "caring".

LEO. Is that weird?

AMANDA. No I'm happy that you're friends.

LEO. Guys aren't allowed to be friends with girls?

AMANDA. C'mon. Of course they are. Look at us. We're friend-ish.

LEO. Well I *was* also looking for a way out of football.

(*Awkward silence.*)

AMANDA. Why don't we go back to the dance.

LEO. Yeah good idea.

(**LEO** *gives an inquisitive look, freezes. Our narrators return, rapidly asking questions:*)

ELINA. Why do some guys always fall for unavailable girls?

AMANDA. Why do some girls fall for the guys who fall for those girls?

ELINA. If you knew what was behind the shadow would you still chase it?

AMANDA. And if you try to tame a lion, is it still a lion anymore? When you're a dancer, these are the kind of things that spin in your mind while doing your morning stretches.

ELINA. Fast forward! Fast forward.

LEO. OK. I think I have the first half down!

(**LEO** *starts to demonstrate in slow motion.*)

LEO. It's left. Left, then back, then turn.

AMANDA. Pirouette.

LEO. I mean pirouette. Then the crazy kick thing.

AMANDA. A cabriole.

LEO. Whatever it's called. But I'm doing it right? Right?

AMANDA. Technically yeah but –

LEO. I suck at this.

AMANDA. Don't be too hard on yourself.

LEO. What's the point?

AMANDA. It's the tip of your toe when you arch your foot.

LEO. I mean the point "of dance." At least in football somebody *wins.*

AMANDA. I think – the point is to try your hardest and not at all at the same time.

LEO. How does that make sense?

AMANDA. You have to *let go* and let your body guide you but at the same time, focus on the goal, on the precision of your movement. Care and not care both at once.

(She demonstrates.)

LEO. Are you implying I care *too* much?

AMANDA. Maybe about certain things.

(They dance in unison. LEO's eyes open – to AMANDA.)

LEO. Yeah. Maybe you're right.

AMANDA. What you're doing right now isn't so bad.

(They dance together. In slow motion.)

LEO. You mean trying not to care?

AMANDA. Yeah that's some really good – not caring you're doing.

LEO. You too.

AMANDA. Gee, thanks.

(SARAH walks in. She watches them dancing, inches from one another. She walks out hurt without being seen.)

ELINA. We all saw it coming…But Sarah saw it first.

(GUZMAN enters decked out in sweatbands.)

GUZMAN. OK. I'm ready to do this!!!

AMANDA. Meanwhile Elina had her hands full with the other one.

ELINA. All you have to do is stand there and lift us. That's it.

GUZMAN. *(waiving his hands)* Hey. That's what these bad boys were made for!

ELINA. You're sure you got this?

GUZMAN. I'm ready.

ELINA. Just grab our hips when we run by. It should look like we're floating.

GUZMAN. Roger that.

ELINA. You ready?

MAYA. Five six seven eight.

(*Cue music.* **ELINA** *tries to go across the room.* **GUZMAN** *tries to hold her hips. He throws her a little too hard.*)

GUZMAN. There she goes.

JOIE. I'm coming. Look out!

(*He tosses* **JOIE**. *He grabs a little too hard.*)

GUZMAN. Whups.

JOIE. Watch where the hand goes!

GUZMAN. My bad.

(**MAYA** *runs by. He misses her.*)

GUZMAN. Shoot. I forgot you existed.

(**ELINA** *turns off the music.*)

ELINA. Guzman. Focus!

GUZMAN. Sorry! Can we do it again?

ELINA. We can't be relying on you in the middle of a show and you forget one of us.

GUZMAN. I know!!! It's just a lot to take in at once!

MAYA. What if we just danced *around* him like he was a tree stump?

JOIE. Or a rock. Maybe he could even be sitting.

MAYA. Or laying flat on his face.

GUZMAN. I'm going to get this right, I promise!

(**JAZ, JESSIE, SARAH** *and* **LIZ** *enter.*)

JAZ. How's it going?

GUZMAN. I'm still trying to get the hang of things.

JAZ. Jessie and Liz have been co-creating the choreography for the finale with Sarah. We're ready to start teaching it to the group. Do we have everyone here?

MAYA. Everyone except Amanda.

JOIE. And Lee-uh-oh.

*(Eyes are on **SARAH**.)*

JAZ. Should we start without them?

SARAH MASTERS. I don't care.

JAZ. Liz, you want to walk them through the opening sequence?

LIZ. You know? Why don't we let Jessie do it?

JESSIE. Really?

LIZ. There's enough dance to go around for everyone.

JESSIE. Sarah, will you help me demon-start?

SARAH MASTERS. Yeah sure.

*(**AMANDA** and **LEO** enter laughing. [They should ad lib some lines about something they both find funny.])*

LEO. What's going on in here?

MAYA. Sarah and Jessie are going to demonstrate their choreography.

SARAH. You count off this time?

JESSIE. Five. Six. Seven. Eight.

*(In slow motion – **JESSIE** and **SARAH** dance.)*

ELINA. Now I've seen a lot of dance in my time. But something about that number. Well. It was like -

*(**LEO** talks to the audience during the slow-motion dance.)*

LEO. It was everything Amanda was trying to explain.

*(**AMANDA** enters too.)*

ELINA. It was raw emotion expressed through movement.

LEO. Manifesting what words could never inspire.

AMANDA. It was like years of restriction unbolting from his limbs.

ELINA. His hands kept growing like vines, scaling her body.

AMANDA. And she was a hundred year-old building; a tower of mortar, breaking down into morsels of sand.

JOIE. I mean you could clearly see she was going through it.

MAYA. Like her parents were breaking apart right before our eyes.

AMANDA. She was breaking apart.

LEO. And she was expressing it all through dance! It was the first time I understood *why people do this.*

AMANDA. Why he was here.

MAYA. Why anyone was, really.

JOIE. It wasn't just for her…it was –

(The music cuts out. **SARAH** *hugs* **LEO***.)*

LEO. Sarah?

JESSIE. You OK?

SARAH. Yeah.

LEO. That was amazing.

SARAH. Thanks.

LEO. I've never seen anyone move like that.

SARAH. I have to go.

(Actors freeze.)

AMANDA. Apparently, we had it all wrong. It wasn't Leo who was in love with Sarah Masters.

ELINA. It was Sarah who was in love with Leo.

(Unfreeze.)

ELINA. *(to* **LEO***)* Go on. Chase her down.

*(***LEO** *catches up to* **SARAH***.)*

LEO. Sarah!

SARAH. What.

LEO. Where are you going?

SARAH. What do you care?

LEO. What's the matter with you?

SARAH. I don't have a problem with you in the company Leo but I do have a problem with you shoving what's going on with you and Amanda in my face.

LEO. Nothing is happening.

SARAH. C'mon. You two are obviously into each other.

LEO. I don't understand. I *joined* the company so I could be there for you but it's like you don't want me anywhere near you.

SARAH. Leo, I didn't want you coming into the Dance Company not because I don't *like* you. It's because I knew everyone else *would*. I know I don't have ownership over you. You're my friend. But these past six months my life has been one big freaking "kick-ball-change". So I would appreciate if you just focused on the only thing that actually makes me feel better right now.

LEO. Just tell me what that is and I'll do it.

AMANDA. The spring show is in three days. Don't make us look bad…

(She walks off. LEO turns around. There's JAZ.)

JAZ. Don't let us down, Leo. Remember. There is no I in "Dance Company".

LEO. No there isn't, is there…

(They freeze.)

AMANDA. OK. Fast forward fast forward fast forward.

ELINA. I admit he practiced a lot.

AMANDA. He was in the dance studio day and night.

ELINA. He was trying his hardest.

AMANDA. But keeping it loose at the same time.

ELINA. Cut to the night of the show.

AMANDA. The auditorium is packed.

ELINA. Every student from Northern Academy is in the audience.

AMANDA. And they're all screaming and extra rowdy this year. Because everyone is talking about how Leo Kogan is about to make his big debut in The Dance Company.

(From behind a curtain:)

LEO. Guys. I really don't know if I can do this.

GUZMAN. You and me, buddy.

LEO. Everyone from the football team is watching. I'm sweating like a monkey and I haven't even started moving.

AMANDA. Just follow my lead if you lose your place.

LEO. What if I freeze up?

AMANDA. Remember what I told you. Focus and relax. Try and let go at the same time.

JOIE. It's dance time, boys.

LEO. Time to get our Cab-Cabaret on, Guzman.

GUZMAN. Hopefully if I just sort of move my arms around and kick my feet they won't realize I have no idea what I'm doing.

LEO. Here goes nothing…

(*LEO* dances the Cab-Cabaret with the company. *ELINA* and *AMANDA* continue to narrate.)

ELINA. He was *horrible.*

AMANDA. Which was amazing.

JOIE. Because good wasn't the point.

MAYA. The point was –

AMANDA. – Is –

LIZ. – to be who you are.

JOIE. And to share who that is.

(*They finish the dance.* **AMANDA** *hugs* **LEO**.)

LEO. I can't believe I did that.

SARAH. How do you feel?

LEO. Great, actually!

SARAH. Seriously. You did great, Leo.

LEO. Yeah. Well. I didn't want to let the company down.

SARAH MASTERS. I think someone wants to congratulate you.

(*Reveal* **AMANDA**, *waiting.*)

SARAH. Go for it.

AMANDA. You did it!

LEO. I didn't try too hard?

AMANDA. Trust me – definitely didn't look like it.

LEO. So you're saying I looked like an idiot.

AMANDA. You were perfectly imperfect.

LEO. Thanks for teaching me how to dance.

AMANDA. It's been an honor to share the stage with you.

(**AMANDA** *looks away.*)

LEO. I think I understand why I joined Dance Company.

AMANDA. Why is that?

(*He kisses her.*)

ELINA. Take it to the changing room.

GUZMAN. Wait. You forgot to tell them what happened with *me*!

ELINA. So Guzman gets on stage. And the girls are coming for their lifts, one by one. And –

(**GUZMAN** *successfully lifts the girls.*)

GUZMAN. Booya! I did it! Best. Dancer. Ever!

(*He raises his fit in the air, victoriously.*)

End of Play

Flip Turn

A Natatorial Fantasia for
8 Swimmers and 2 Lifeguards

Madeleine George

FLIP TURN premiered with Keen Company (Jonathan Silverstein, Artistic Director), as part of Keen Teens Season 7, at Theatre Row in New York City on May 3, 2013. The performance was directed by Larissa Lury, with sets by Collin McGurk, costumes by Amanda Jenks, lighting by Jeffrey Toombs, and sound by Colin Whitely. The Production Stage Manager was Alex H. Hajjar. The cast was as follows:

RILEY	Arnab Baig
ANDERSON	Sheikhar Boodram
PROFESSOR GLOEKNER	Hasheem Brin
MORRIS	Alyssia Marte
LOU	Erica Ohmi
OLIVIA	Alyssa Powell
ARTIS	Jelaya Stewart
DYLAN	Victor Torres
SHELL	Shanique Williams
MERLE	Karla Ynfante

CHARACTERS

OLIVIA, 17
DYLAN, 16
SHELL, 28
RILEY, 36
MORRIS, 48
ANDERSON, 31
ARTIS, 32
PROFESSOR GLOECKNER, 45
LOU, 56
MERLE, 80

TIME

Present

SETTING

Underwater and on deck at the Highland City Pool

NOTES

Swimsuits aren't necessary. Neither are fake swimming moves – ideally, the language should do the swimming. Movable lane dividers or backstroke flags might help. All prop/set/costume solutions, whatever they are, should be broadly indicative, theatrical, cheap, and low-tech.

There was no line, no roof or floor
to tell the water from the air.

— Maxine Kumin, "Morning Swim"

(In black: Ocean. Great waves breaking on a vast beach.)

(Recedes into: the echoey squeak and splash of a public pool.)

(A rush of bubbles.)

(Lights up underwater. Shimmery aquamarine world.)

(Eight lanes. In each lane, a swimmer. They swim in the metronomic rhythm of laps – consistent, monotonous. Each to his or her own steady beat.)

(We watch them from below.)

(On opposite sides of the pool, topside, only dimly visible to us through the water, **OLIVIA** *and* **DYLAN** *amble back and forth on deck in red T-shirts and sport shorts, red rescue tubes slung across their chests like messenger bags. They both carry whistles.* **OLIVIA** *wings hers around her finger, unwinds it, wings it back the other direction.)*

(They are blurry, silent, and far away.)

MORRIS. Don't be intimidated by the flip turn. It's not as acrobatic as it sounds. Just think of it as rolling into a ball, not flipping. Just rolling into a ball. Not flipping. Not flipping.

RILEY. No one can see me.

No one can see me.

LOU. I'm not asking you,

I'm telling you.

ARTIS. I'm a gladiator.

I'm a killer.

LOU. I'm not asking you,

I'm telling you.

RILEY. No one can see me.

ARTIS. No one walks away from a fight with me alive.

RILEY. No one can see me.

SHELL. The water will heal me.

RILEY. The water completely conceals me.

ARTIS. In the hell-octagon of the Human Resources Department, I am the ultimate fighting *champion.*

ANDERSON. And Phelps pulls out to an early lead.
Chasing history, going for a record nineteenth gold.

PROFESSOR GLOECKNER. *(toneless murmur-singing)*
IT'S THE EYE OF THE TIGER
AND THE THRILL OF THE NIGHT

(**ANDERSON** *and* **PROFESSOR GLOECKNER** *'s thoughts braid together, overlap.*)

ANDERSON. Look at that loping stroke.

Look at the *wingspan* on that guy.

PROFESSOR GLOECKNER. rising up to the huh-huh of survival

ANDERSON. This is the moment the whole pool has been waiting for.

This is the moment the whole world has been waiting for.

PROFESSOR GLOECKNER. and the spider around you is the chill of the fight and the *luh* duh duh *hum* duh duh EYE *(pause)* of the tiger

ANDERSON. This crowd is on its feet, Jim.

They're bursting at the seams.

All eyes are on Phelps.

They are screaming his name.

RILEY. No one can see me.

MERLE. *(with effort – alternately self-coaching and grimacing with pain)* Reach!
and!
RATS!
and!

Reach!

and!

OUCH!

and!

SHELL. The water washes me like a ritual bath.

The water holds me in a gentle embrace.

It surrounds and suffuses me.

It restores my soul.

PROFESSOR GLOECKNER. muh muh muh My Sharona

MERLE. I'm stiff as a –

Reach!

– corpse.

Rats!

My shoulder's on –

Ouch!

– fire.

Crap!

When they fish me out of here with the giant –

Reach!

– net I hope they call Doctor "Swimming is the Safest Exercise" Schmidt –

Ugh!

to come down here and personally –

Reach!

– pronounce me –

OUCH!

– dead!

CRAP!

MORRIS. Keep your head in line with your body.

Center yourself on top of the T.

Gain momentum as you approach the wall. Kick. Harder. The more momentum you have, the cleaner your turn will be.

As you flip, bring your eyes and knees together into a tuck. Bring your heels in towards your buttocks.

MORRIS. *(cont.)* Blow air out your nose. Don't be intimidated. Now accelerate, accelerate –

(Big group inhale.)

(A rush of bubbles.)

(FLIP.)

(Topside. On deck.)

(DYLAN approaches OLIVIA. This is the first time he's ever crossed a room to talk to a girl he hasn't already met before.)

(They both face mostly out as they talk, scanning their zones of surveillance as instructed to by the Red Cross Lifeguarding Manual.)

DYLAN. If you'd rather have the chair you can totally –

OLIVIA. No that's cool, I like standing.

DYLAN. Oh, okay. Cool.

(Pause.)

I'm Dylan.

(He'd offer his hand for her to shake, but somehow he can tell she wouldn't touch it. Gives a little wave instead.)

OLIVIA. Hey.

DYLAN. Hey.

(Pause.)

(simultaneous) So you're new here –

OLIVIA. *(simultaneous)* Is that guy Steve a total –

(They halt. Try again.)

DYLAN. *(simultaneous)* Go ahead.

OLIVIA. *(simultaneous)* You go.

DYLAN. No you go, you go, what?

OLIVIA. Is that guy Supervisor Steve a total asshat?

DYLAN. Um...

OLIVIA. 'Cause first of all who calls themself "Supervisor Steve"? And then he gave me this insanely condescending five-hour lecture about how to use the timecard machine, and I was just like yes I *know*, I kept being like, yes I have seen one of these mechanisms *before* Steve, I operated one like four times a week for an entire *year*.

DYLAN. Oh, that sucks. Yeah, I don't know, he's okay. Sometimes he doesn't trust you. Because we've had, like, incidents with the staff, is I guess why.

OLIVIA. *(now she's interested)* Seriously? Like what kinds of incidents?

DYLAN. Like nothing serious, just like, I don't know, I wasn't involved in them or anything, but just this one scam a couple of guys pulled where one guy would punch the other guy's card and make it look like there were two guards on deck during open swim when actually one guy was out back by the Dumpsters dealing drugs out of his van.

OLIVIA. Wow.

DYLAN. Or something like that, I don't really know, I wasn't involved, I just heard about it. The cops came and everything.

OLIVIA. Intense.

DYLAN. Yeah. That guy Goldfarb, who was like the ringleader or whatever? He was a total douche. I mean I barely even talked to the guy. He once called me a
– *(shrug)*. Whatever.

OLIVIA. Who Goldfarb? I knew a kid named Goldfarb. He was a badass.

DYLAN. Yeah, James I think?

OLIVIA. My kid was Kenny.

DYLAN. Oh. That must not have been the same Goldfarb, then.

OLIVIA. *(duh)* No.

(Pause.)

DYLAN. I mean, it was definitely totally badass and intense what they did, but it's also like, technically a violation of rule nine point four to have only one guard on deck with more than six patrons in the pool, so like, it wasn't exactly safe.

OLIVIA. *(sarcasm)* Not to mention drugs can kill.

DYLAN. *(missing her tone completely)* Right, right, totally, I know! And not that I wanted to see Goldfarb and Cho and Rathgaber get fired or anything, I was personally totally fine working with those guys, but it was actually kind of a relief when they left, and also it opened up slots for some new people to come in. Like you.

OLIVIA. *(neutral)* Yeah.

DYLAN. Which is nice.

OLIVIA. *(tentative)* Yeah.

DYLAN. Didn't you use to work up at Renard Street Aquatics?

OLIVIA. *(wary)* Yeah.

DYLAN. Yeah I saw you there. Once or twice I think. I used to train there. Before.

(Rush of bubbles.)

(FLIP.)

(Underwater.)

MORRIS. Okay, no problem. Next time. Next time. Every length of the pool is another opportunity to try the flip. Don't be intimidated. Next time's the charm.

RILEY. Everyone's focused on themselves. No one's thinking about me.

PROFESSOR GLOECKNER. *(toneless murmur-singing)*
    BUM BUM CHA
    BUM BUM CHA

MORRIS. The first time you do something, it's always terrifying.

RILEY. I'm in my own orbit. I'm alone in the universe.

PROFESSOR GLOECKNER. singin

> WE WILL WE WILL
>
> ROCK YOU
>
> *(pause)*
>
> BUM BUM

MERLE. I may already be dead. After all, I'm doing the dead man's float.

LOU. You wanna die right here on the Midtown Express?

MERLE. No, dead man's float is facedown. I'm belly-up. Dead *goldfish* float.

LOU. Because it can be arranged, my friend.

PROFESSOR GLOECKNER.

> BUM BUM CHA

RILEY. If no one can see me, no one can hurt me.

LOU. *(contained rage)* Rule of thumb for interacting with other human beings: don't assume you have a clue what's going on inside their heads.

PROFESSOR GLOECKNER.

> ROCK YOU

LOU. *(with escalating rage)* Anyone you meet could be at the end of their rope. Anyone you meet could have spent the last eighteen years of their life kissing Roger from Management's ass and putting in eighty-hour weeks so they no longer have any social life to speak of, only to find that the firm is picking up and moving to Cleveland and they're taking the opportunity to trim the fat. And I'm the fat. Eighteen of the best years of my life and I'm the *fat*. So, my young friend in the puffy vest and giant headphones, don't assume I'm willing to accept from you the same disrespectful treatment I tolerated for eighteen years from Roger. I may not have a right to a career, I may not have a right to basic human happiness, but I have a *right* to the four square feet of personal space around my body, ordained by God and Thomas Jefferson as my birthright on this planet. So when I say excuse me, when I say will you please move your bag that is apparently full of gold ingots off the delicate bones of my foot, I am not *asking* you, I am *telling* you, Mister Vest, and if you do not respond I will take my ballpoint pen and plunge it through your vest into your cold, stupid heart with the full force of eighteen years of pent-up rage. And cheerfully leave you to bleed out on the floor of the Midtown Express.

PROFESSOR GLOECKNER.

BUM BUM CHA

ARTIS. Downsizing's happening. Either Javier goes, or I go. Can't do it by seniority 'cause we both got hired the same week. One of us has to outperform the other.

PROFESSOR GLOECKNER.

BUM BUM CHA

ARTIS. I may like the guy. I may consider him a friend. But I have no choice but to destroy him.

PROFESSOR GLOECKNER.

ROCK YOU

ARTIS. We used to get lunch together. He took his decaf black. He liked Milky Ways. That's nice, but those details mean nothing to me now. I scrub them from my memory. From now on he's not Javier, guy from the next cubicle who likes Milky Ways and has a slideshow of pictures of his Yorkie, Maurice, as his screensaver. From now on he is my *prey*. He is *meat* to me. Dead, cold meat.

MERLE. Would it be so terrible to be dead?

ARTIS. It's not personal. It's just business.

MERLE. Let's say I kill myself. Accidentally. Say I overdo it and buy the farm right here in the shallow end. When you come right down to it, wouldn't it be a relief? Sciatica? Poof. Arthritis? Poof. Empty apartment with no one but Oprah to say hello to me when I come in the door? *(little pause)* What is there to be afraid of, really?

PROFESSOR GLOECKNER. *(toneless operatic warbling)* O mio
babbino caro
mi piace nell OOOOOOOOO
seeeeeeno

SHELL. The water doesn't wash the memories away.
The water lets them float inside my mind, easy, gentle.
The water holds me the same way the universe holds
her, forever and ever.

PROFESSOR GLOECKNER. *(quiet)* vendaaaa nel popee roso
ni piace bel anelllllooooooo

SHELL. In the beginning, we were all swimmers. We floated
in a tiny sea. And in the end we'll float away again,
swept out on the cosmic tide. When a soul goes from
the first ocean to the final ocean without ever stepping
on dry land, the water is the best place to find her
again. She's close to me underwater. I'm swimming
here, she's swimming in eternity.

MERLE. I bet being dead's a lot like going swimming.
Although hopefully with more flattering outfits.

SHELL. The water will heal me.

PROFESSOR GLOECKNER. Mi piace dell
OOOOOOOOOO
seeeeeeeno

MORRIS. Start your flutter kick. When you're half a body's
length away, tuck your forehead into your belly button
and bring your knees to your forehead. Let your hands
float, weightless, as you tumble over. Place your feet on
the wall and spring off like a rocket. Easy.

ANDERSON. Jim, this guy makes it look so easy. And he
has a day job, too? Did I hear that right? That's right,
Hal. Not many people know this, but Michael Phelps
manages to compete internationally while still holding
down a job as a frozen team leader for a midsize
supermarket. I'm sorry, Jim, but how is that possible?
How does a world-class athlete like Phelps manage to
live two totally separate lives? How does he find time

to *train*? On his lunch hour, Jim. What an inspiring story! This just keeps getting better and better!

ARTIS. Every human being I meet is a competitor. *(ARTIS notices **ANDERSON** in the next lane over.)* Like you, buddy. You think you're fast?

MORRIS. Fast. Look down. Trust.

ANDERSON. What a great role model for aspiring athletes everywhere!

ARTIS. You think you're the champ? I'll destroy you. I'll show you hydrodynamic. You think you're leading the heat, but I'm about to lap you in five, four –

MORRIS. – trust –

ARTIS. – two –

(Big group inhale.)

(A rush of bubbles.)

(FLIP.)

(Topside. On deck.)

DYLAN. Um so, you used to date that guy, didn't you, what was his name?

OLIVIA. How do you know who I used to date?

DYLAN. Um, because you guys would make out a lot in the lifeguard station at Renard Street? Or I thought it was you guys, I don't know, maybe it wasn't.

OLIVIA. Me and that guy aren't together anymore.

DYLAN. Oh. Uh-hunh.

OLIVIA. I don't really want to talk about it, actually.

DYLAN. Oh. Sure.

(Little pause.)

OLIVIA. *(to change the subject)* What about you, you have a boyfriend or girlfriend or something?

DYLAN. *(quick)* Girlfriend? Girlfriend? I like girls?

*(**OLIVIA** shrugs heedlessly.)*

OLIVIA. Whatever, I'm open-minded, I don't care either way.

DYLAN. No, me too, I don't care either, but it's *girlfriend*. *(small pause)* It would be girlfriend. I don't have one.

OLIVIA. Yeah? You're lucky.

DYLAN. *(dubious)* Yeah?

OLIVIA. Of course. You're seriously better off alone. Relationships are a nightmare. *(taking him to school)* You give everything you have to a person, everything precious in your heart and soul and then you loan him two hundred dollars of your own saved-up money so he can buy a used Spider Jam 75 Watt amp that he allegedly needs to cut his demo or whatever and then he lets Ella Simonson do things to him in a 7-Eleven parking lot and you *never see that two hundred dollars again.*

DYLAN. Oh. Man.

OLIVIA. That's what I call a violation of trust.

DYLAN. Yeah.

OLIVIA. It's like, let's say I trust you. Let's say your name is "Dylan," or whatever, and you and me are –

DYLAN. *(overlapping)* My name *is* Dylan.

OLIVIA. *(pleased with herself)* Oh, did I just guess that?

DYLAN. No, I told you.

OLIVIA. *(mildly disappointed)* Oh. I thought I made it up.

DYLAN. No, I introduced myself before.

OLIVIA. Oh. *(she assesses him)* You *kind* of look like a Dylan. A little bit, around the chin. Really you look more like a Kevin.

DYLAN. My cousin's name is Kevin.

OLIVIA. *(super bored with that piece of information)* Uh-hunh. So what was I saying?

DYLAN. Um –

OLIVIA. Oh right, let's say I *trust* you, and your name is Dylan and I trust you because we're going out or whatever and I say to you Hey Dylan, let's go get frozen yogurt on Thursday after school but until then can you please not let any other girls touch your wang? And you're like, yes, absolutely, it's a deal, but then on *Wednesday* you let Ella Simonson do things to you in a 7-Eleven parking lot, how am I supposed to believe anything you say anymore?

DYLAN. Totally.

OLIVIA. How am I supposed to believe anything *anyone* says? Ever?

DYLAN. Right.

OLIVIA. That's what I call getting your heart broken. Or another way to put it is getting screwed over.

DYLAN. Yeah.

OLIVIA. I mean, whatever. It is what it is. I had to transfer from Renard Street to here even though this place is totally inconvenient for me to get to and there aren't even vending machines in the break room here because I couldn't stand to be near him anymore, not even for one more shift.

DYLAN. That sucks.

OLIVIA. Yeah, it actually really does suck. It sucks having to drive here and it sucks not having vending machines but most of all it sucks to realize that it's not possible to trust another person, ever, at all. I don't even trust my *mom* anymore. She *loved* Derek. She was all, "One mistake shouldn't doom an entire relationship." I was like, Whose mom *are* you? It was so effed up.

(**DYLAN** *nods thoughtfully.*)

DYLAN. That does sound…that does sound really effed up. But also I wonder if it's like, really true.

OLIVIA. *(extremely hostile – "what's true?")*
     What?

DYLAN. Just, that we can't trust anyone besides ourselves. That seems really bleak, don't you think?

OLIVIA. *(last call, swirling her fourth martini)* Welcome to the world, "Dylan."

DYLAN. But like, I mean, look at all these people. *(DYLAN sweeps the pool with his arm)* They trust us.

OLIVIA. They don't even know us.

DYLAN. True but they trust us 'cause we're their lifeguards. They trust us to perform our duties according to the regulations of the Red Cross manual, which we were trained on and which we know by heart.

OLIVIA. Well maybe they shouldn't trust us. Maybe we're impostors. Maybe we barely even read the manual.

(DYLAN laughs.)

DYLAN. *(amused)* Yeah right! As if we wouldn't have read the manual! We're *certified.* And they know that. That's why they can come here and be like, Okay, I'm just going to dive into this pool and swim, because I know that the water's been tested for pathogens, and the right proportion of chlorine to bromine has been calibrated, and the temp and the pH are at appropriate levels, and the rules are being enforced for everyone's safety, and I don't have to worry about anything, even drowning, even *death*, I can totally forget all my fears and just get in a really great workout today because the guys in the red T-shirts are *on it.* They're keeping me safe. *(he smiles)* I always feel so happy standing on deck looking out at all these people swimming, knowing that they don't have a care in the world, because I've got everything under control.

(OLIVIA regards DYLAN with some distaste.)

OLIVIA. You're kind of an egomaniac.

DYLAN. What? No I'm not, I'm just saying –

OLIVIA. *(cutting him off)* I'm sorry but you kind of are. You look all timid or whatever on the outside, but inside you're like extremely conceited. You think you took these people's fear of *death* away by putting on a T-shirt and reading a pamphlet about bee stings?

DYLAN. *(passionate)* That is – first of all, the manual is about *way* more than just bee stings, and it's not a *pamphlet*, it's a really important, really thick book about how to save lives and how to handle emergencies that –

OLIVIA. *(overlapping)* Dude, all I know is you came sauntering over here invading my personal space, talking about how you can save people from death and hitting on me in the middle of my shift on my first day here and –

DYLAN. *(overlapping – shocked)* I am not – I am not hitting on you!

OLIVIA. Oh yeah? Asking me about my boyfriend which is a totally obvious move and also none of your business and also probably a violation of rule number nine point whatever about preventing sexual harassment in the workplace, I should probably report you to Supervisor Steve for asking me that question –

DYLAN. *(overlapping)* I was not – wait no please don't report me to Supervisor Steve, I'm sorry if I was sexually harassing you but if I was it was a total accident, I was just trying to get to *know* you 'cause you're new here and you seem nice and –

(The air and water begin to merge.)

MORRIS. Don't be intimidated.

OLIVIA. For a second there I thought you were different, but you're just like every other guy. You're not trustworthy.

DYLAN. I am so!

RILEY. Don't worry what anyone else is thinking.

OLIVIA. You think you're superman but you're all talk and no action.

DYLAN. I wasn't trying to be all talk and no action, I was trying to be proactive and Change the Script and Make Something Happen In My Life like my mom said!

MORRIS. Don't look ahead to where you're going. Just trust.

OLIVIA. Whatever. It doesn't matter.

DYLAN. Wait, I'm sorry! I'm sorry.

MERLE. I'm tense.

SHELL. I'm merged with the water.

ARTIS. I'm a killer.

MORRIS. I'm bold.

MERLE. I'm stiff.

LOU. I'm not kidding.

MORRIS. I'm fearless.

RILEY. I'm invisible.

ANDERSON. I'm invincible.

PROFESSOR GLOECKNER. *(murmured pizzicato)*
  I'M STARTING WITH THE MAN IN THE MIRROR...

SHELL. I'm ninety-eight percent water.

MORRIS. I'm accelerating. Accelerating. I trust that the wall is there. Faster. I trust.

(Collective inhale.)

(Rush of bubbles.)

(FLIP.)

*(Lights darken. Night sky. **MORRIS** begins to drown.)*

(slow, dazzled) Oh: I'm tumbling. Ink up my nose. Ink all around me. Space all around me. Space up my nose. It all happened so fast. I had no idea I was a cosmonaut. I had no idea I had it in me. Feet are for walking, I always thought, but then I sprang off them like a rocket and now look: when I kick, I make plumes in the stardust. Deep and high at the same time. *(a wonderful realization washes over **MORRIS**)* Oh, *I* get it. *I* get it now. No problem. It's okay with me that it's all the same.

(Distant, blurry din from the other side.)

RILEY. *(muffled, distant)* Look! Hey look! Don't you see what's happening over here?

(MORRIS jerks upwards, blurts out a huge noisy cloud of bubbles.)

(crushed with disappointment)

RILEY. *(cont.)* Oh no, no, no, I love it up here, don't drag me down. Let me stay space walking. Let me stay falling.

(Rush of bubbles.)

(FLIP.)

(Topside. Emergency.)

(DYLAN has hauled MORRIS out onto the deck. MORRIS lies on the deck, eyes closed. DYLAN and OLIVIA crouch over. The swimmers crowd around.)

DYLAN. Back up. Back up. Give us space, please.

MERLE. Oh my God.

SHELL. Oh my God.

ANDERSON. Oh cripes.

RILEY. I knew something was wrong!

DYLAN. *(to OLIVIA)* We need to intitiate a resuscitation response. *(to the swimmers)* Swimmers, please don't crowd the victim!

(The swimmers take a group step back.)

(MERLE leans in front of LOU to peer at MORRIS.)

MERLE. I knew somebody's number was up today, I just thought it was mine.

LOU. *(to MERLE; hostile)* Excuse me.

MERLE. *(sarcastic)* Oh, I'm sorry, am I crowding you? You need a front-row seat to the autopsy?!

SHELL. Autopsy?

(SHELL steps back from the group. PROFESSOR GLOECKNER notices SHELL back away.)

OLIVIA. Resuscitation response? Shouldn't we do CPR? Or call Steve, or –

DYLAN. Trust me. Resuscitation response.

OLIVIA. Okay. Okay.

(**DYLAN** *goes to retrieve a breathing mask.*)

(*leaning down and shouting into* **MORRIS***'s face*)

CAN YOU SPEAK? CAN YOU SPEAK?

DYLAN. Dude, that's the Heimlich!

OLIVIA. I'm sorry! I've never been in an actual emergency before!

DYLAN. Just sound the EAS, I'll commence mouth-to-mouth.

(**DYLAN** *places the breathing mask over* **MORRIS***'s mouth and nose.*)

OLIVIA. *(hiss whisper)* What's an EAS?

DYLAN. Emergency Action Signal?

OLIVIA. I don't know what that is! I barely read the manual!

DYLAN. Just blow your whistle!

OLIVIA. Okay, okay!

(**OLIVIA** *blows her whistle.*)

(*The pool falls silent.*)

(**DYLAN** *inhales – we hear it as if it is an elemental wind, filling the entire building.*)

(**DYLAN** *exhales into the breathing mask in* **MORRIS***'s mouth. Huge, cavernous breath.*)

(**MORRIS***'s chest rises.*)

(**MORRIS** *coughs convulsively, spits out the breathing mask, sits up.*)

OLIVIA. *(stunned)* You did it.

RILEY. Oh thank God.

ARTIS. Oh thank God.

ANDERSON. Amazing. Nice work.

DYLAN. *(to* **MORRIS***)* Are you all right?

MORRIS. *(to* **DYLAN***)* I wasn't drowning.

OLIVIA. You were totally drowning.

MORRIS. I was turning.

DYLAN. You were in severe respiratory distress.

MORRIS. I was finally doing it.

DYLAN. We just need you to stay seated until we're able to confirm your vitals and make sure you're fully recovered. And then we'll have you fill out an incident report.

MORRIS. Okay.

DYLAN. Everyone, the victim has been stabilized, we are out of phase one of the emergency. But please hold off on continuing your workouts until I have notified the supervisor and two guards are present on deck. We'll sound the whistle to let you know when it's safe to re-enter the water.

(**OLIVIA** *and* **DYLAN** *separate off from the group.*)

I'm going to notify Steve. You keep an eye on the victim and make sure nobody gets back in while I'm gone.

OLIVIA. Okay, yeah. We wouldn't want to be in violation.

(**DYLAN** *goes to leave, but* **OLIVIA** *checks him.*)

Hey. You handled that so amazingly.

DYLAN. I just followed the manual.

OLIVIA. Whatever, it was totally badass and intense.

DYLAN. Thanks.

OLIVIA. My hands are shaking.

(**DYLAN** *looks down at his hands.*)

DYLAN. Yeah. Mine too.

(**DYLAN** *exits.*)

(*The swimmers have been conferring.*)

ANDERSON. *(to* **ARTIS***)* You want to keep going when they let us back in?

ARTIS. Keep going…what?

ANDERSON. Weren't you racing me in there? I loved it! I loved how you were egging me on, pushing me to achieve. What do you swim, a one-minute fifty? You're a gladiator, man.

ARTIS. I…thanks.

ANDERSON. You're like Phelps. *(***ANDERSON*** checks that* **ARTIS** *knows him)* Michael Phelps? America's greatest athlete?

ARTIS. I've heard of him.

ANDERSON. You've got Phelps's sportsmanship, too. It takes courage to make an overture like that to a stranger, in a whole nother lane, to reach out and say, hey, let's team up to pursue some *excellence* together.

ARTIS. Well I do love…excellence.

ANDERSON. We should train together, maybe. I'm here every day from twelve to one.

(**ARTIS** *smiles.*)

ARTIS. Okay.

ANDERSON. Let's stay limber so we're ready to hit the blocks the second they blow the whistle. You know, there's a right way and a wrong way to warm up your hams.

(**ANDERSON** *leads* **ARTIS** *to the edge of the pool. They stretch to stay warm.*)

MERLE. *(to* **LOU***)* I'm sorry about crowding you. I was just cold, really. Huddling.

LOU. *(awkward)* It is chilly out here.

MERLE. Chilly, it's *freezing*! I can't do this cold/warm, cold/warm – I get a cramp when I go from one to the other too quick. It makes me chesty, too. (**MERLE** *coughs, demonstrating)* And at my age, this morning's chest cold is this afternoon's pulmonary embolism.

(**MERLE** *coughs again.*)

(LOU considers MERLE, de-towels, drapes the towel around MERLE's shoulders.)

LOU. Here. You don't want to catch your death.

MERLE. Thanks.

(PROFESSOR GLOECKNER and SHELL.)

PROFESSOR GLOECKNER. It rattled you a little.

(SHELL nods.)

I saw.

SHELL. I don't know if I can get back in. I know the water's not the enemy, but...I need to feel like I'm safe in there, like it's protecting me, not trying to kill me. But how can I give up swimming? It's the only thing that keeps me sane.

PROFESSOR GLOECKNER. I've always been deathly afraid of the water. What I do when I swim, is I sing. Keeps up a nice rhythm. Focuses the mind. Helps me forget that I'm a big, warm-blooded mammal with no fins or flippers, flopping around in the element made for fish.

(SHELL smiles.)

SHELL. I don't sing.

PROFESSOR GLOECKNER. You don't have to carry a tune.

(PROFESSOR GLOECKNER starts to sing in a lovely voice – lucid, vivid, on pitch.)

ROW ROW ROW YOUR BOAT
GENTLY DOWN THE STREAM
MERRILY MERRILY MERRILY MERRILY
LIFE IS BUT A DREAM

(After a moment, SHELL joins in.)

(SHELL and PROFESSOR GLOECKNER sing quietly under the following.)

(RILEY sits beside MORRIS.)

RILEY. You were going back and forth and back and forth, and then I saw you kind of floating upside down by the wall and I thought, that's not right. Something's not right with that person.

MORRIS. I didn't know anyone could see me.

RILEY. I could. *(small pause)* I always thought if no one could see me, I'd be safe. But if I hadn't seen you…

MORRIS. I'd be in Davy Jones' locker. *(small pause)* I saw you, too. You have a nice stroke.

(RILEY blushes.)

RILEY. I'm an amateur.

MORRIS. We're all amateurs.

(Little pause.)

RILEY. What were you doing down there?

MORRIS. Flip turn.

RILEY. Like in the Olympics?

(MORRIS shrugs.)

MORRIS. Just a regular flip turn. My first. *(MORRIS thinks)* I didn't have to try it. I had a perfectly good routine, thirty-two lengths, open turns, three times a week. But I always knew I *wasn't* doing the flip. And I started to think, not trying this is ruining me. There's a new world waiting for me on the other side of this thing, I know it, and I have to get there or die trying. It was dangerous, more dangerous than I knew. I almost didn't make it. But it was wonderful.

(DYLAN reenters.)

DYLAN. Swimmers, thank you for your patience. It is now safe to enter the water.

(The swimmers take their marks at the edge of the pool.)

(DYLAN steps into place, rescue tube at the ready.)

(OLIVIA steps into place, rescue tube at the ready.)

(DYLAN blows his whistle.)

(Big group inhale.)

(Lights fade.)

(Ocean. Great waves breaking on a vast beach.)

End

A Polar Bear
In New Jersey

Anna Moench

*A **POLAR BEAR IN NEW JERSEY*** premiered with Keen Company (Jonathan Silverstein, Artistic Director), as part of Keen Teens Season 7, at Theatre Row in New York City on May 3, 2013. The performance was directed by Shelley Butler, with sets by Collin McGurk, costumes by Amanda Jenks, lighting by Jeffrey Toombs, and sound by Colin Whitely. The Production Stage Manager was Alex H. Hajjar. The cast was as follows:

ICE FLOE	Helen Barnes
TEACHER	Marietou Bokoum
KELLY	Cameron Davis
JESSICA	Kimberly Giles
AVINNAQ	Paola Guerini
OFFICER FINLEY	Ralphie Irizarry
SARAH	Chanel Kinery
PRINCIPAL GRANGER / MOM	Heavenly Martinez
ROCKY	Oddisey Miller
MRS. FINLEY	Joy Sunday
ROCCO / LINDSEY	Paolo Valdez

CHARACTERS

ICE FLOE – An ice floe. Our narrator. (M or F)

AVINNAQ – A three year old polar bear. Three in bear years = 16 in human years. (F)

MOM – An adult polar bear. (F)

ROCKY – A raccoon. (M)

ROCCO – A raccoon. (M)

OFFICER FINLEY – An adult black bear. Local police officer. (M)

MRS. FINLEY – An adult black bear. City Councilbear of Bearville, NJ. (F)

JESSICA FINLEY – A three year old black bear. Athlete. (F)

PRINCIPAL GRANGER – An adult black bear. Principal of Bearmont High School. (F or M)

TEACHER – A forgetful adult black bear. (F or M)

SARAH – A three year old black bear. The most popular cub in school. (F)

KELLY – A three year old black bear. Sarah's lackey. (F)

LINDSEY – A three year old black bear. Sarah's lackey. (F)

OTHER STUDENTS – As many as needed. (F or M)

*Note on doubling: There are many doubling possibilities with this script, and groups are encouraged to double as needed. The minimum number of actors needed is 8, with the following doublings: Mom/Teacher/Principal Granger, Rocky/Kelly, Rocco/Sarah, and Mrs. Finley/Lindsey. The maximum number can be as high as 13, with additional actors playing Other Students who can ad-lib lines in the classroom scene. Actor gender is flexible in all of these characters due to the stylized nature of the play.

Scene One

(Lights up on a bare stage. An **ICE FLOE** *drifts onstage slowly. Very, very slowly. It smiles at the audience.)*

ICE FLOE. Hey guys. Thanks for making the trip tonight, it's great to have you here. You have a lot of places you could be, but you chose to be here. And that means a lot to all of us here in the Arctic Circle.

(The **ICE FLOE** *continues to drift across the stage.)*

Speaking of which, welcome to the Arctic Circle! Alaska! The last frontier! Everybody comfy? Anybody need a blanket? Too bad, I don't have free blankets for every rando who shows up. If you're chilly, snuggle up to your neighbor. Get cozy. Cause you're gonna be here a little while.

I'm an ice floe. My job is to float around, getting bigger when it gets colder and getting smaller when it gets warmer. Yo-yo dieting, what a drag, am I right, ladies?

But as I think we all know by now, it's been getting warmer a lot more than it's been getting colder these days. At first I was like "Sweet, look at my tiny butt!" and I bought a bunch of new jeans. But I just kept shrinking, and now I'm too small to wear them.

(The **ICE FLOE** *gets caught in an eddy and starts slowly spinning around.)*

Crap. Eddy. I hate it when I get stuck in these. Uh…all right, this could take a while guys, bear with me.

(The **ICE FLOE** *continues to rotate slowly.)*

Well, anyway, I brought you guys here because it seems like I'm going to keep shrinking and shrinking until I'm…well. Gone. Which sucks. But. That's life. Change is inevitable, they say, as much as we all hate it. We had

65

a good thing going, up here in the frozen north. I'll be
sorry to see myself go.

But before that happens, I wanted to be sure I had the
chance to tell someone this story. A story about a polar
bear. A story about our changing world. It all started
on Avinnaq the polar bear's third birthday...

*(The arctic sea is replaced by a suburban living room
with a white couch and coffee table. It's quiet. After a
few moments, some keys in the lock. The front door opens
and* **AVINNAQ** *enters.* **AVINNAQ** *is a polar bear.)*

AVINNAQ. Mom? I'm home! No luck out there. I swear, it's
like, every time I go on a hunt the ice shelf is closer
and closer, like it's melting or something. I dunno. It's
probably just in my head.

*(***AVINNAQ*** flops down on the couch.)*

Anyway, the hunting's been the pits. Whenever I get
close to a seal the ice cracks apart underneath me and
I fall into the water! Maybe I'm too heavy.

*(***AVINNAQ*** looks at herself in the mirror. She tries to suck
in her belly.)*

Nah. I look great.

*(***AVINNAQ*** notices the silence.)*

Mom?

*(***AVINNAQ*** starts looking around the house. She comes
across a note on the coffee table, picks it up, and reads.)*

*(***MOM*** appears in a pool of light somewhere on the stage.)*

MOM. My dearest Avinnaq,

Today is your third birthday. It seems like only yesterday
you were rolling around in the snow den with me,
your little eyes fused shut. But time flies, and now it's
time for you to find your own family. I've left you my
compass.

*(***AVINNAQ*** picks up a compass from the coffee table.)*

My mother gave it to me to help me find my way when I was three, and now it's yours. I dropped it a few times, but I'm sure it still works.

Love,

Mom.

AVINNAQ. Oh my god.

MOM. P.S. I'm sorry I had to leave you without saying goodbye in person, but I didn't think I could bear it. Get it? BEAR it?

AVINNAQ. That's not funny.

MOM. Yes it is.

Scene Two

(ICE FLOE is still spinning in the eddy.)

ICE FLOE. And so, Avinnaq set off on her journey, guided by her mother's compass.

(AVINNAQ enters, peering at the compass.)

AVINNAQ. Okay, compass! My fate is in your hands. Help me find a new place to live, where I can dig a snow den and start my own family. Hmm. It looks like north is…that way!

(AVINNAQ points offstage and starts marching in place. A stagehand pulls a strip of white fabric across the stage, making it look like AVINNAQ is walking across the snow.)

ICE FLOE. It wasn't. But the compass was the only friend Avinnaq had left in the whole world. So she followed its advice, even as the snow gave way to grass…

(The white fabric becomes green fabric. AVINNAQ looks down at it, confused. She checks her compass, shrugs, and keeps marching.)

And grass gave way to mountains…

(A mountain flat is wheeled across the stage, AVINNAQ dodges it and keeps marching.)

And mountains gave way to plains.

(Light brown fabric is pulled across the stage. AVINNAQ marches on.)

There's a fine line between persistence and insanity. But that's a debate for another day.

So just when Avinnaq was starting to think she would never see another bear again, just when she was starting to doubt her mother's compass – uhh, ya think? – Just when she thought she might have to turn back…

(A sign is rolled onstage. It says "WELCOME TO NEW JERSEY!")

Scene Three

*(**ROCKY** and **ROCCO**, a pair of raccoons, are going through a trashcan.)*

ROCKY. So I says to the guy, I says, if you can't take the heat, get out of the attic! Then I peed on 'im.

(Both raccoons crack up, laughing long and loud. They wipe their eyes and keep rummaging through the trash.)

Exterminators. Please. Buncha amateurs.

ROCCO. So you and Marcy are still up in that attic on French Street?

ROCKY. Yeah, it'll take more than a guy in a beige jumpsuit to get rid of us. Marcy's just had the litter, so it's not a good time to relocate. That said, soon enough the kits are gonna need some more space, so who knows.

ROCCO. They grow so fast at that age.

ROCKY. Tell me about it. I come home in the morning after a long night of foraging and they're like twice as big as when I left!

*(**AVINNAQ** leaps out from behind some trash cans with a roar and pins **ROCKY** down with her enormous paw. **ROCCO** screams and runs away.)*

ROCCO. POLICE! POLICE! HELP!

ROCKY. I surrender! Take whatever you want, it's all yours, here, I got some expired Ding Dongs and some pizza crusts, they're yours, just please, don't hurt me! I gotta wife and 3 kits at home!

*(**AVINNAQ** raises her paw to kill **ROCKY** in one swipe.)*

ROCKY. No! Okay, okay, I was hiding the Flamin' Hot Cheetos powder, take it! Take anything you want!

*(The lights of a police squad car light up the stage. **AVINNAQ** looks around, confused. **OFFICER FINLEY**, a black bear, enters with a megaphone, gun drawn. **ROCCO** is at his side.)*

ROCCO. That's her, Officer! The big white monster!

OFFICER FINLEY. THIS IS THE POLICE. YOU ARE UNDER ARREST. RELEASE THE RACCOON AND TURN AROUND WITH YOUR PAWS UP.

ROCKY. You heard him! Release the raccoon!

AVINNAQ. What's a raccoon?

ROCKY. I'M a raccoon, ya bully!

OFFICER FINLEY. IF YOU DO NOT COMPLY IMMEDIATELY, WE WILL BE FORCED TO SHOOT.

AVINNAQ. But I'm hungry.

ROCKY. Hungry??

(**OFFICER FINLEY** *takes aim.*)

OFFICER FINLEY. THIS IS YOUR FINAL WARNING. RELEASE THE RACCOON OR I WILL SHOOT.

(**ICE FLOE** *pops in.*)

ICE FLOE. Don't worry guys. It's only a tranquilizer gun. They may be bears, but they aren't animals.

(**ICE FLOE** *exits.*)

AVINNAQ. Tell you what, how about I just kill this raccoon thing first, and then we'll talk. He's making a lot of noise.

(**OFFICER FINLEY** *shoots* **AVINNAQ** *with a tranquilizer dart.*)

OW! Hey, that wazn't…verry…nice…

(**AVINNAQ** *stumbles and falls to the ground, releasing* **ROCKY**, *who scurries off with* **ROCCO**. **OFFICER FINLEY** *approaches her. Blackout.*)

Scene Four

(AVINNAQ wakes up in a tiny cell, more like a kennel than a room. She tries to move, but can't.)

AVINNAQ. Ow. Stupid police.

Stupid compass.

Stupid Mom.

Stupid me.

(OFFICER FINLEY approaches the cell.)

OFFICER FINLEY. You're up.

AVINNAQ. Yeah, so?

OFFICER FINLEY. You're in the Bearmont town prison. Aggravated assault.

AVINNAQ. Assault?

OFFICER FINLEY. Raccoon by the name of Rocky. Decent guy. Family man. You should be ashamed of yourself.

AVINNAQ. But he was snack sized.

OFFICER FINLEY. ...you're not from around here, are you.

(AVINNAQ and OFFICER FINLEY continue talking, silently. The ICE FLOE drifts back onstage.)

ICE FLOE. Hey guys! Check it out, I'm out of the eddy!

(The ICE FLOE gets trapped in another eddy.)

Crap.

Okay, well, Avinnaq and Officer Finley got to chatting, and Avinnaq told him all about her life in the Arctic, her bittersweet birthday note from her mom, and her long journey to find a new home...

AVINNAQ. ...and that's when I saw the raccoons.

OFFICER FINLEY. So you kill other animals for your food?

AVINNAQ. Of course.

OFFICER FINLEY. *(looking around furtively)* Shh!

(OFFICER FINLEY approaches the cell and speaks to AVINNAQ quietly.)

OFFICER FINLEY. *(cont.)* Look. If you want to make this your new home, you can't say things like that. We're suburban bears. Murder has no place in a civilized society, and our laws reflect that.

...You know, I have a daughter who's about your age, just turned three, getting close to graduating from high school.

AVINNAQ. Are you about to kick her out?

OFFICER FINLEY. What? No! We don't do that here.

AVINNAQ. Wow. I wish you were my dad.

OFFICER FINLEY. Oh. Thank you. That's very nice of you to say.

(**AVINNAQ** *shrugs.* **OFFICER FINLEY** *looks at her.*)

I think this whole assault charge should be dropped. You didn't know any better.

AVINNAQ. Really?

OFFICER FINLEY. Really. I'll talk to Rocky. He owes me one anyway, I've let him off the hook for public urination more times than I should admit.

(**OFFICER FINLEY** *lets* **AVINNAQ** *out of the cell. She stretches to her full height.*)

Wow. You're...impressive.

AVINNAQ. Am I free to go?

OFFICER FINLEY. Yes. But here's the thing. You're in Jersey now. You can't just go around mauling every animal in town that's smaller than you. Because honestly, that'd be every animal in town.

AVINNAQ. But what can I eat?

OFFICER FINLEY. Why don't you come over for dinner with my family tonight. We'll show you what you've been missing out on.

Scene Five

(MRS. FINLEY and JESSICA are at the Finley home.)

JESSICA. Mooomm, I'm staarving.

MRS. FINLEY. Your father will be home soon, sweetheart.

JESSICA. Whatever, let's just go.

MRS. FINLEY. This family eats dinner together. You know that.

JESSICA. This family's stupid.

MRS. FINLEY. Jessica.

JESSICA. Sorry. I told you, I'm starving. I barely have control over what I'm saying.

(OFFICER FINLEY opens the front door and enters.)

OFFICER FINLEY. There are my girls!

MRS. FINLEY. Hi honey!

(OFFICER FINLEY gives MRS. FINLEY a kiss on the cheek.)

OFFICER FINLEY. How was your day?

MRS. FINLEY. Busy. My constituents in the state park are furious, apparently the park service installed bear proof food bins for the campers. Without their votes, I'm not sure I can win this election.

OFFICER FINLEY. Well, if anyone can figure it out, you can.

JESSICA. Let's GO. My stomach has practically digested my intestines already.

(AVINNAQ enters. MRS. FINLEY and JESSICA scream.)

SASQUATCH! SASQUATCH!

MRS. FINLEY. Brian, do something!

OFFICER FINLEY. Everybody just calm down. This is Avinnaq. She's new in town, and I invited her to stay with us a few nights while she gets her bearings.

ICE FLOE. *(poking its head onstage)* Heh. BEARings.

(ICE FLOE leaves.)

OFFICER FINLEY. Avinnaq, this is my wife, Mrs. Finley, and my daughter, Jessica.

AVINNAQ. Hi.

MRS. **FINLEY**. Oh. Dear. I'm so sorry, Avinnaq, you just…I wasn't expecting any visitors.

(whispering)

Brian, you could have called. This is a very busy week, what with my election coming up, and Jessica's game on Friday…

OFFICER FINLEY. She needs a place to stay, Helen.

MRS. **FINLEY**. But –

OFFICER FINLEY. Let's talk about this later. Who's hungry?

JESSICA. Me!

AVINNAQ. Me too!

JESSICA. *(to her* **MOM**, *under her breath)* Isn't she big enough already?

MRS. **FINLEY**. Jessica. That is rude and uncalled for.

OFFICER FINLEY. I think we'll all feel a lot better once we eat something. Come on.

(The bears exit the house.)

Scene Six

(**OFFICER FINLEY, MRS. FINLEY,** and **JESSICA** stand by several overturned trash cans, having already eaten their fill. They are watching **AVINNAQ**, whose entire front end is buried in a trash can. The sounds of happy slurping and chewing emanate from the trash can.)

JESSICA. Gross.

OFFICER FINLEY. Jessica.

JESSICA. What? You guys always pick on me about my trashcan manners!

MRS. FINLEY. It's not polite to point out a guest's…mistakes.

OFFICER FINLEY. Avinnaq doesn't know any better. She was raised in the Arctic Circle. They don't have trash cans up there.

JESSICA. Then how do they eat?

OFFICER FINLEY. Uh…Avinnaq dear? Can we get you anything else?

(**AVINNAQ** burps loudly. **AVINNAQ** emerges, licking her paws.)

AVINNAQ. You were right, Officer Finley. This is way better than –

OFFICER FINLEY. How about I get you another can?

AVINNAQ. Bring it on!

(**OFFICER FINLEY** exits.)

MRS. FINLEY. So Avinnaq. Which school are you going to enroll in?

AVINNAQ. Oh, I don't go to school.

MRS. FINLEY. But you have to go to school.

AVINNAQ. Why?

MRS. FINLEY. Because that's the law.

AVINNAQ. You guys sure have a lot of laws.

(**OFFICER FINLEY** returns, rolling a trash can in front of him.)

MRS. FINLEY. Brian, we were just talking about where to enroll Avinnaq in school.

OFFICER FINLEY. Why doesn't Jessica bring her to Bearmont tomorrow?

JESSICA. What??

MRS. FINLEY. Are you sure that's the best place for her…

AVINNAQ. FOOD!

(**AVINNAQ** *rips the lid off the trash can and dives in with gusto.*)

OFFICER FINLEY. Of course! Jessica can show her around, introduce her to the other cubs, it'll be great.

JESSICA. MOM!

MRS. FINLEY. It's just…Jessica's big game is the day after tomorrow, and she shouldn't have any distractions. Besides, I think Avinnaq may have…special needs.

OFFICER FINLEY. Are you serious?

JESSICA. Duh, Dad. Look at her.

(**AVINNAQ**, *stuck inside the trashcan, is rolling around on the ground.*)

MRS. FINLEY. Not "special needs", but she does have some special needs. The poor cub has never been to school before. She could barely feed herself without our help.

OFFICER FINLEY. She may not have gone to a traditional school, but she's a smart cub. She'll be fine.

JESSICA. I'm not showing her around.

OFFICER FINLEY. If you want to play in the Bearball game on Friday, you are.

JESSICA. Dad! It would be social suicide!

OFFICER FINLEY. Then get up on that bridge.

(**AVINNAQ** *manages to extract herself from the trash can.*)

AVINNAQ. Anybody wanna go halfsies on dessert?

Scene Seven

(The school. JESSICA *and* AVINNAQ *arrive early, before the other students. They're alone.)*

JESSICA. *(looking around to see that the coast is clear, and walking quickly onstage)*
Hurry up! Come on!

AVINNAQ. What's the rush?

JESSICA. Nobody's here yet, and I want to get you off my back before that changes.

AVINNAQ. But you're supposed to show me around all day.

JESSICA. Yeah, like that was ever gonna happen. The principal will find some sucker to do that. Come on, her office is down here.

*(*AVINNAQ *stops and points out toward the audience.)*

AVINNAQ. What are those?

JESSICA. Lockers.

AVINNAQ. What are lockers?

JESSICA. You put stuff in them.

AVINNAQ. What stuff?

JESSICA. I dunno, like books and stuff.

AVINNAQ. What are books?

JESSICA. Are you kidding me with this? Come on!

*(*JESSICA *grabs* AVINNAQ*'s arm and pulls her along.* PRINCIPAL GRANGER *appears in front of them, wearing a t-shirt that says* GO BEARS!*.)*

PRINCIPAL GRANGER. Hello, Jessica.

JESSICA. Oh, hi Principal Granger!

PRINCIPAL GRANGER. What do we have here?

JESSICA. This is Avinnaq. She's new in town.

PRINCIPAL GRANGER. Well well well! It's such a pleasure to have you with us, Avinnaq! It'll do wonders for our diversity statistics.

JESSICA. I thought maybe you could find someone to show her around.

PRINCIPAL GRANGER. Good idea! Let's see, who do we have…

(PRINCIPAL GRANGER *looks around the empty hallway. It's empty. She looks back down at* JESSICA, *who is trying to edge away.*)

What about you, Jessica?

JESSICA. Me? Oh, no, you should really give it to someone more…responsible.

PRINCIPAL GRANGER. Nonsense! I can think of no better bear to represent Bearmont than our bearball star herself! Avinnaq, it was a pleasure to meet you. I'm leaving you in Jessica's capable paws.

AVINNAQ. What's bearball?

PRINCIPAL GRANGER. What's bearball? What's bearball??

JESSICA. It's not a big deal, really.

PRINCIPAL GRANGER. It is a HUGE deal! Every school in the state picks its best student to compete in a one on one game that relies on agility, speed, and strength! This year, Jessica has made it all the way to the championship.

AVINNAQ. What do you get if you win?

PRINCIPAL GRANGER. We get to know we're better than those snobs at St. Beary's. We're all counting on you, Jessica! GO BEARS!

(PRINCIPAL GRANGER *exits, and the bell rings. Students swarm in.*)

JESSICA. Come on, let's go to homeroom before anyone sees us.

(JESSICA *and* AVINNAQ *make their way through the crowd.* AVINNAQ *attracts a lot of attention, and pretty soon everyone has stopped what they're doing to stare at her.* SARAH *approaches, flanked by* KELLY *and* LINDSEY.)

SARAH. Hey Jessica.

JESSICA. Hey Sarah. Hey Kelly. Hey Lindsey.

KELLY. Hey.

LINDSEY. Yeah. Hey.

SARAH. You ready for the big game on Friday?

JESSICA. Totally. We're gonna destroy St. Beary's.

SARAH. Last year you choked in the final quarter. Everyone was pretty pissed at you.

KELLY. So pissed.

LINDSEY. Crazy pissed.

SARAH. That must have been embarrassing for you.

KELLY. So embarrassing.

LINDSEY. Crazy embarrassing.

SARAH. And in case you're wondering, that's why I didn't invite you to my birthday party last year. It was fun.

KELLY. So fun.

LINDSEY. Crazy fun.

JESSICA. Well I'm better this year.

SARAH. Well you better be.

JESSICA. Well I am.

SARAH. Well good.

KELLY. Yeah, good.

LINDSEY. Good.

JESSICA. Yeah.

SARAH. Well, maybe if you don't screw it up, you can come to my party this year.

JESSICA. Really?

SARAH. Maybe.

JESSICA. That would be cool.

SARAH. Of course it would. It's the coolest party ever.

KELLY. So cool.

LINDSEY. Crazy cool.

SARAH. So. Who's your friend?

JESSICA. Oh, she's not exactly my –

AVINNAQ. I'm Avinnaq!

> (SARAH *looks* AVINNAQ *up and down. She turns back to* JESSICA.)

SARAH. What kind of a name is that?

AVINNAQ. It's Inupiaq.

SARAH. What does that even mean.

AVINNAQ. It's my language.

SARAH. Why are you hanging out with this freak show?

AVINNAQ. Hey!

JESSICA. *(looking between* AVINNAQ *and* SARAH*)*
Um…I'm…she's…I'm not hanging out with her. She's been following me around.

AVINNAQ. But Jessica, you're supposed to –

JESSICA. Get away from me, sasquatch!

> (*People giggle.*)

SARAH. Ha! I get it. Sasquatch! Because you're fat, and white, and ugly!

KELLY. So fat!

LINDSEY. So ugly!

SARAH. Good one, Jessica!

> (*Everyone starts to laugh.*)

AVINNAQ. I'm not a sasquatch! That's not even a real thing!

EVERYONE. Sasquatch! Sasquatch! Sasquatch! Sasquatch!

> (AVINNAQ *growls. The bell rings. Everyone goes to class.* JESSICA *and* AVINNAQ *are alone in the hall.*)

JESSICA. Sorry about that. It's just…those cubs…whatever, never mind. Come on.

> (AVINNAQ *follows* JESSICA *off.*)

Scene Eight

(Homeroom. The students are sitting in chairs. **AVINNAQ** *is standing awkwardly at the front of the class next to the* **TEACHER**.*)*

TEACHER. All right class, let's give a big Bearmont High welcome to our newest student, Annievack!

AVINNAQ. It's Avinnaq.

TEACHER. Annavack.

AVINNAQ. Avinnaq.

TEACHER. Sorry. Annavick.

(Snickers from the class. **AVINNAQ** *sighs and goes to her chair.)*

SARAH. Careful, Sasquatch. Don't break the chair.

*(**AVINNAQ** ignores her and sits down.)*

TEACHER. Ok, let's get started. Where are my glasses…

*(**SARAH** makes a farting noise. She pinches her nose and points at* **AVINNAQ**.*)*

SARAH. EWWWW!

(Everyone moves their desks away from **AVINNAQ**.*)*

TEACHER. *(finding glasses)*
Ah, here they are. Now. Today we've got a pop quiz… oh. Shoot. Where are the quizzes? I must have left them in the copier.

(The **TEACHER** *exits, muttering to herself.)*

SARAH. That was gross.

AVINNAQ. That wasn't me.

SARAH. So what are you, anyway?

AVINNAQ. I'm a polar bear.

SARAH. I thought polar bears were extinct.

KELLY. Totally extinct.

LINDSEY. Like, dead.

AVINNAQ. We're not extinct.

SARAH. But isn't your habitat melting away because of global warming?

AVINNAQ. What's global warming?

(People start to giggle.)

SARAH. Do you really not know what global warming is?

AVINNAQ. No, what is it?

SARAH. Oh my god, are you, like, stupid or something?

(Everyone starts to laugh. **AVINNAQ** *looks around.* **JESSICA** *avoids eye contact.* **AVINNAQ** *is close to tears.)*

AVINNAQ. I have to go to the bathroom.

SARAH. Why, are you gonna fart again?

AVINNAQ. No.

SARAH. Sasquatch, Sasquatch, sitting in a tree, F A R T I N G!

*(***AVINNAQ*** leaves the classroom.)*

JESSICA. Leave her alone, Sarah.

SARAH. Excuse me?

JESSICA. Just…whatever, who cares about her anyway?

SARAH. Seems like you do.

JESSICA. What? No I don't.

SARAH. Yeah you do.

KELLY. You totally do.

LINDSEY. You crazy do.

SARAH. You're like in LOVE with her!

JESSICA. Ew, shut up!

SARAH. You like wanna have a bunch of sasquatch babies with her!

KELLY. A thousand sasquatch babies.

LINDSEY. A million sasquatch babies.

JESSICA. No I don't!

SARAH. Then prove it.

KELLY. Yeah, prove it.

LINDSEY. Yeah.

(Everyone is staring at **JESSICA**.*)*

JESSICA. Fine.

*(***JESSICA*** gets out her smartphone and types something into it.)*

*(***AVINNAQ*** re-enters, drying her eyes.)*

Okay, sasquatch. This is from Wikipedia.

AVINNAQ. What's Wikipedia?

(Everyone laughs.)

JESSICA. Just listen. Rising temperatures are causing sea ice to disappear for longer and longer periods, leaving polar bears insufficient time to hunt. Unless the pace of global warming slows or stops, polar bears could disappear within a century.

AVINNAQ. That's not true!

JESSICA. It is.

AVINNAQ. It's not! It can't be!

JESSICA. Polar bears are history!

AVINNAQ. *(standing to her full height)* No we aren't!

JESSICA. I bet your mom drowned in a melted iceberg!

(The **TEACHER** *reenters just as* **AVINNAQ** *roars and swipes* **JESSICA** *with her enormous paw.* **JESSICA** *falls to the ground. The other students scream and run out of the classroom.)*

TEACHER. HELP! HELP! SOMEONE CALL THE POLICE!

Scene Nine

(The Finley home. **OFFICER FINLEY** *and* **MRS**. **FINLEY** *are sitting together in silence.)*

OFFICER FINLEY. You can't do this!

MRS. **FINLEY**. We need to get rid of her, Brian. She's different from us, she's a wild animal.

OFFICER FINLEY. We're all wild animals! She just hasn't had a chance to adjust yet. There is no reason to kick her out, everyone is overreacting.

MRS. **FINLEY**. Why are you so intent on protecting her?

OFFICER FINLEY. Someone has to.

MRS. **FINLEY**. And what about your daughter? Who's going to protect her?

(JESSICA enters. Her arm is in a sling.)

JESSICA. Mom? Can you get me something to eat?

MRS. **FINLEY**. Sure, sweetie. I'll bring back a couple of trash cans for you.

JESSICA. From the houses in the cul de sac? They're my favorite.

MRS. **FINLEY**. Of course. Go back to bed.

JESSICA. I won't be able to play in the game tomorrow. They gave me another shot after I screwed up last year, and now I'm gonna let them all down again.

MRS. **FINLEY**. Don't worry about that right now. It's not your fault.

(JESSICA exits. **MRS**. **FINLEY** *looks at* **OFFICER FINLEY**.*)*

You know whose fault it is, Brian.

*(**OFFICER FINLEY** sighs.)*

I can't force you to agree with me, Brian. But the town is demanding action, and I can't just stand idly by.

OFFICER FINLEY. Because you're scared of losing the election.

MRS. FINLEY. So what if I am? It's my job to do what the bears of this town want.

OFFICER FINLEY. No, it's your job to do the right thing.

MRS. FINLEY. Yes. And the right thing to do is get rid of that monster before she hurts another cub.

(*MRS. FINLEY exits. OFFICER FINLEY puts his head in his paws.*)

(*The ICE FLOE drifts onstage again.*)

ICE FLOE. Officer Finley didn't know what to think. One the one paw, Avinnaq was just a cub. She was sweet, and trusting, and she really didn't know any better. On the other paw, she was a freaking POLAR BEAR. She was about twice the size of even the biggest, burliest black bears, and she was a stone cold killer! What's a father to do?

So. Officer Finley went into the yard, where Avinnaq was waiting, and gave her a trash can and a blanket.

(*OFFICER FINLEY goes outside to AVINNAQ.*)

OFFICER FINLEY. I'm sorry, Avinnaq, but you'll have to stay out here tonight.

AVINNAQ. Is Jessica okay?

OFFICER FINLEY. She will be.

AVINNAQ. I feel really bad about what I did.

OFFICER FINLEY. I told you, Avinnaq. Things are different here, we have laws. It's not okay to hurt other animals.

AVINNAQ. But they hurt me. They hurt my feelings.

OFFICER FINLEY. Hurting feelings isn't against the law. Hurting someone's body is.

AVINNAQ. Why aren't they both against the law?

OFFICER FINLEY. ...I don't know. Maybe they should be. But they aren't.

(*OFFICER FINLEY exits back into the house, and offstage.*)

ICE FLOE. Night came, but Avinnaq couldn't sleep. She felt terrible about what had happened. Even though that melted iceburg thing was totally over the line. I mean. I am literally melting as we speak. How would you like it if I came to your house and melted you down, and then joked about how your mom was gonna…drown in your…melty…juices. Or whatever. You know?

AVINNAQ. …You're really reaching on that one.

ICE FLOE. Shh, just don't think about it too hard.

Anyway, to distract herself, Avinnaq picked up a ball that was lying around and started playing with it.

(**AVINNAQ** *picks up a fish-shaped ball and starts playing with it, tossing it around and bouncing it.*)

Upstairs, Jessica couldn't sleep either. She too felt terrible about what had happened. But then she heard the familiar sounds of a bearball being pawed.

(**JESSICA** *comes out of the house and watches* **AVINNAQ**.*)

JESSICA. Hey.

AVINNAQ. Oh. Hey.

(*They stare at each other for a while.*)

JESSICA. You're really tall.

AVINNAQ. Enough with the sasquatch jokes, okay?

JESSICA. No, I mean, I bet you're practically the height of the bearball hoop.

(**AVINNAQ** *looks up at the bearball hoop, strung with a fishing net. She stands to her full height. It's within reach.*)

JESSICA. Wow.

(**AVINNAQ** *sits back down again.*)

AVINNAQ. How's your arm?

JESSICA. It's okay.

(*Silence.*)

JESSICA. It's just those cubs. Sarah and Kelly and Lindsey. They're so cool, and everyone wants to be friends with them, and I just…wanted them to like me.

AVINNAQ. Why? They're awful.

JESSICA. Yeah, but that's why you want them to like you. So they won't be so mean to you.

AVINNAQ. Huh.

JESSICA. Now that I'm articulating this, it doesn't actually make that much sense.

AVINNAQ. I wasn't going to say anything.

JESSICA. Sorry.

AVINNAQ. Thanks.

Sorry I swiped you.

JESSICA. I was kinda asking for it.

AVINNAQ. Yeah, but the game. Your team has to forfeit. It sucks. I just wish I could do something to make it up to you.

(Silence.)

JESSICA. Can you dunk?

AVINNAQ. What's dunk?

JESSICA. Can you put the ball through the hoop?

(AVINNAQ stands and dunks the ball easily.)

…I have an idea.

(ICE FLOE appears again, with a microphone. It sings the ROCKY "Training Montage" song into the microphone. JESSICA and AVINNAQ do a training montage.)

(Lights up on JESSICA showing AVINNAQ how to dribble. AVINNAQ keeps dropping the ball.)

(Lights up on JESSICA counting as AVINNAQ does jumping jacks.)

(Lights up on JESSICA showing AVINNAQ how to push opponents out of the way, using trash cans as stand ins. AVINNAQ bowls them all over.)

(Lights up on **JESSICA** *showing* **AVINNAQ** *how to dribble again.* **AVINNAQ** *still drops the ball.)*

(Lights up on **JESSICA** *counting as* **AVINNAQ** *jumps rope.)*

(Lights up on **JESSICA** *holding a carton of eggs. She throws it into a trashcan.* **AVINNAQ** *dives in and eats them.)*

(Lights up on **AVINNAQ** *dribbling the ball like a pro. She takes it to the hoop and dunks.* **JESSICA** *cheers and they high five.)*

ICE FLOE. That's my favorite part.

Scene Ten

(The locker room. The sounds of a crowded gymnasium can be heard through the doors.)

*(***PRINCIPAL GRANGER, OFFICER FINLEY,*** and **MRS. FINLEY** are standing in the locker room. **PRINCIPAL GRANGER** is still wearing her GO BEARS! t-shirt.)*

PRINCIPAL GRANGER. And Jessica didn't say why she wanted us here?

OFFICER FINLEY. No, she just left us a note saying to come to the game.

MRS. FINLEY. I suppose she wants to forfeit to St. Beary's in person, and she needs our support.

PRINCIPAL GRANGER. Oooh, I can't *stand* the idea of forfeiting to that snotty St. Beary's principal. I was really hoping for a win this year, so I could rub it in her prissy little face!

OFFICER FINLEY. Well, there's no way Jessica can play, with her injury.

PRINCIPAL GRANGER. Poor thing. It's such a shame, what happened. But I could tell from the start, that polar bear was no good. Bloodthirsty killers, all of them.

MRS. FINLEY. You'll be happy to know that the city council has passed the Polar Bear Ban. It was a unanimous vote, after what happened to Jessica. I mean really. She barely survived.

*(The **ICE FLOE** pokes its head onstage.)*

ICE FLOE. Get it? BEARly?

*(Everyone glares at the **ICE FLOE**.)*

Yeesh. Tough crowd.

*(The **ICE FLOE** leaves.)*

PRINCIPAL GRANGER. Well I, for one, am very relieved. We can all sleep a lot more soundly now.

*(**JESSICA** and **AVINNAQ** enter.)*

JESSICA. Hi everybody!

PRINCIPAL GRANGER. MONSTER!

MRS. FINLEY. Get away from her, Jessica! What's wrong with you!

JESSICA. No, it's okay, Mom. Avinnaq's sorry, and she's making it up to me by playing the bearball game against St. Beary's today! As long as that's okay with you, Principal Granger. If not, I can always forfeit. And you can go out there and shake paws with the principal of St. Beary's. And we can accept defeat. Again.

PRINCIPAL GRANGER. Hmm. Well, everyone's already here expecting a game...it would be a shame to disappoint them...

JESSICA. Great! Here, Avinnaq, you can wear my lucky jersey.

MRS. FINLEY. I'm sorry, but I think you're all forgetting the Polar Bear Ban that was voted into law today. Avinnaq can't play. Technically she can't even be here!

JESSICA. That's not fair!

MRS. FINLEY. It's the law!

AVINNAQ. Again with all the laws!

JESSICA. I can't believe you're doing this!

PRINCIPAL GRANGER. I really want to crush St. Beary's!

OFFICER FINLEY. Hey! HEY! Everybody quiet down! Now look here. As the law enforcement presence, I do have the obligation to enforce whatever laws the city council has passed.

MRS. FINLEY. See?

OFFICER FINLEY. However. Perhaps I could wait to enforce them a little while. Perhaps I could wait even as long as it takes to play a game of bearball.

JESSICA. YES!

MRS. FINLEY. What??

PRINCIPAL GRANGER. Go get em, Avinnaq!

(AVINNAQ puts on JESSICA*'s jersey, which is a little small for her, and stands to her full height. She lets out a mighty roar, and runs off, onto the court.)*

(The ICE FLOE *appears.)*

ICE FLOE. The score was an unprecedented 574 to 0, and after that, the citizens of Bearmont weren't so interested in having Avinnaq arrested. In fact, Bearmont High found a new mascot that day.

*(*PRINCIPAL GRANGER *appears, wearing a t-shirt that says GO POLAR BEARS!)*

PRINCIPAL GRANGER. GO POLAR BEARS! Raaaaaaar!

*(*PRINCIPAL GRANGER *exits.)*

ICE FLOE. Mrs. Finley even won the election, overturning the Polar Bear Ban. Turns out it's very good publicity, having the town hero in your spare bedroom.

*(*MRS. FINLEY *appears, mid-acceptance speech.)*

MRS. FINLEY. – I want to thank each and every one of you for your vote, and I especially want to thank a very special bear for all she did on the campaign trail…

*(*AVINNAQ *enters to riotous applause. Flashbulbs explode in their faces as they smile and shake hands. They exit.)*

ICE FLOE. Jessica decided it wasn't so important to go to Sarah's birthday party after all, now that she was best friends with the coolest bear in school. In fact, pretty much everyone decided it wasn't so important to go to Sarah's birthday party.

*(*SARAH, KELLY, *and* LINDSEY *enter, wearing party hats. They sit alone, bored, in silence for a while.)*

SARAH. This is fun.

KELLY. *(yawning)* So fun.

(A pause. SARAH *and* KELLY *look over at* LINDSEY. *She is asleep, and lets out a big snore.* SARAH *elbows her. She wakes up.)*

LINDSEY. Hmm? Oh. Crazy fun.

(She falls back asleep. All exit.)

ICE FLOE. And that was how a lost polar bear found a home and a family in Bearmont, New Jersey. From that day on, the Finleys and Avinnaq devoted all their free time to protecting the future of the polar bears by backing local legislation to reduce Bearmont's carbon emissions through renewable energy incentives and an improved public transit system.

*(**AVINNAQ**'s rear end is visible as she rolls across the stage in a trash can.)*

Well, almost all their free time. I hope they'll manage to save Avinnaq's fellow polar bears. Whether they'll be able to save me from melting away into the ocean, I'm not sure. But I'm glad you made it up here to hear my story before that happened. Because if the town of Bearmont can change, then maybe the world can change. And if the world can change, then maybe the Arctic Circle won't have to. I'd really appreciate that. At this rate, my next pair of jeans is gonna be coming from the Barbie aisle at the Toys 'R Us. And nobody wants to see that. It was fun hanging out with you. I'll miss you guys. Get home safe.

*(The **ICE FLOE** starts to drift offstage waving goodbye to the audience. It gets caught in another eddy.)*

Crap.

The End